To Sergi , who turns ink characters
into colorful laughter.
José Carlos Andrés

To Luna, my little pirate: never be afraid to do
what really makes you happy.
Sonja Wimmer

The Journey of Captain Scaredy Cat
Somos8 Series

© Text: José Carlos Andrés, 2014
© Illustration: Sonja Wimmer, 2015
© Edition: NubeOcho, 2015
www.nubeocho.com – info@nubeocho.com

Original title: *Los miedos del capitán Cacurcias*
English translation: Amaranta Heredia Jaén y William Vercoutre
Text editing: Martin Hyams

Distributed in the United States by
Consortium Book Sales & Distribution

First edition: March 2015
ISBN: 978 84 943691 4 8
Printed in Spain – Gráficas Jalón

The Journey of Captain Scaredy Cat

José Carlos Andrés

Sonja Wimmer

nubeOCHO

Captain Scaredy Cat

looks like a pirate,

dresses like a pirate,

and roars

YO HO HO!

like pirates do.

Everything shows he's a real

pirate.

Captain Scaredy Cat never

not even of sharks on a stormy night

not of sharks, not of the night, not of storms...

...sed to be afraid of anything:

...e was so daring that not even rancid milk nor girls' kisses scared him. He was the bravest of them all!

Not long ago, and for no special reason, the Captain started to be scared of everything:

the size of his new shoes, the itchiness of his coat and even his own height.

He was also fearful that his crew would laugh at him...

everything scared him.

Even his own shadow!

Captain Scaredy Cat's ship was called "The Angry Shark" and the members of his crew were very rude, tough, and wild.

They loved their Captain very much, but they never told him, because pirates do not talk about their feelings.

When they knew that Captain Scaredy Cat was so scared, they decided to help him.

They thought, and they thought, and they thought...
The only idea they could come up with was
to take him to the Blue-eyed Ghost's ship.

"What horrible help you offer me!" said Captain Scaredy Cat.

The pirates of his crew were very rough
and thinking was not their thing.

When Captain Scaredy Cat was left alone on the ship, what was expected happened: a ghost appeared.

But not any ordinary ghost... it was

THE BLUE-EYED GHOST!

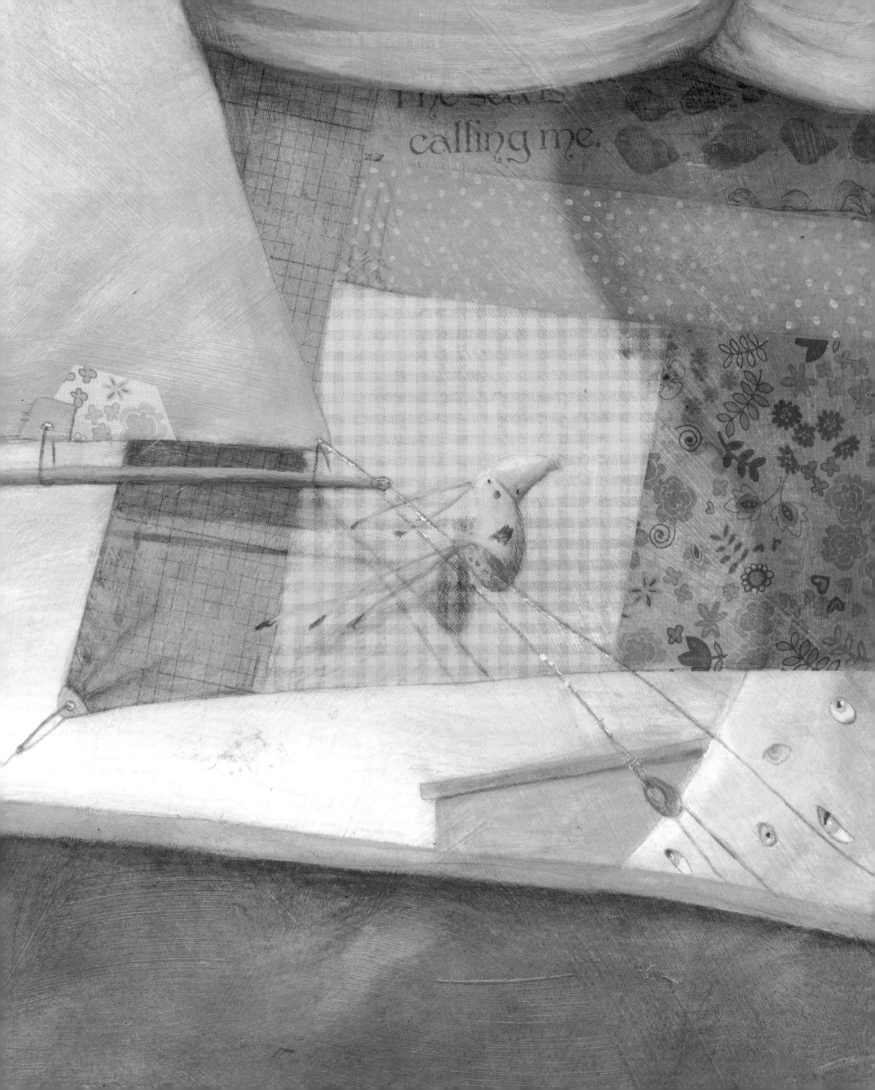

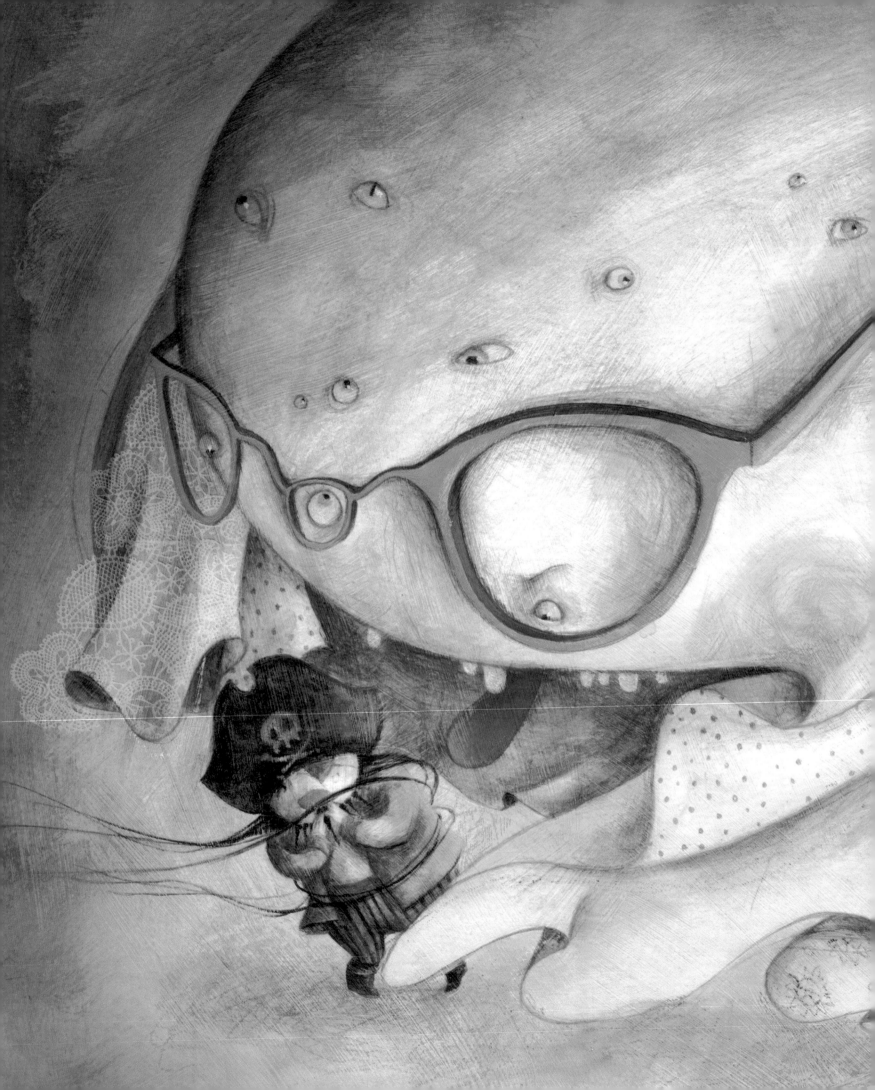

BOO!

screamed the ghost.

Poor Captain Scaredy Cat almost doodied in his pants.

He was so scared that he could not even run. The ghost was getting closer, and closer, and closer...

The pirate shook more than a ferocious lightning flash.

SATURD
Septem

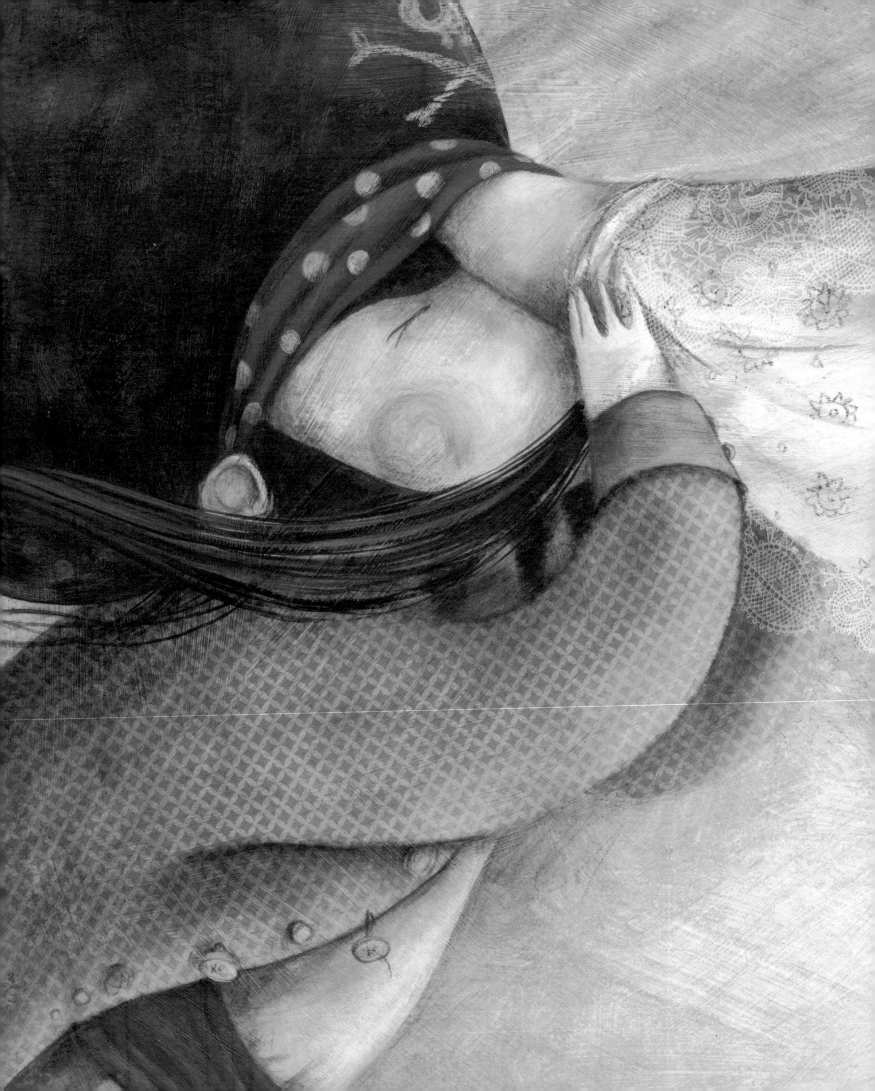

When he could not handle the fear any more, Captain Scaredy Cat
started to think: "Wait a moment...! Do ghosts exist? No! They don't exist!"

And so he shouted out loud:

"They don't exist, they don't exist, they don't exist..."

Then, all of a sudden, the ghost vanished!

Captain Scaredy Cat was just beginning to recover from the shock when something

hideously skinny and whitish,

wearing a black cape,

with long,

sharp fangs appeared:

A VAMPIRE!

YUM, YUM, YUM!

yelled the vampire, showing his teeth with his mouth open.

Captain Scaredy Cat trembled

as the vampire got closer and closer...

so close that the Captain could even smell his garlic breath!

Captain Scaredy Cat thought to himself again: "Do vampires exist?" he whispered, quivering like a paper ship in open sea. "No, of course they don't!"

So he shouted out loud:

"They don't exist, they don't exist, they don't exist..."

And then...

the vampire vanished!

Captain Scaredy Cat started to think that he was imagining everything and decided to explore the haunted ship.

But then, as happens to nosy captains, he came across

something horrific:

a giant,

enormous,

and colossal...

WEREWOLF!

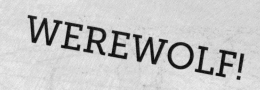

RAR, RAR, RAR!

barked the werewolf.

The creature was ugly, ugly, ugly... truly ugly.

Worst of all, he was full of fleas
and looked enraged.
The creature was getting closer.
And so were the fleas.

He was so close, that one flea bit
Captain Scaredy Cat's big toe.

And the Captain started to think again:
"Wait a moment, wait a moment...
Do werewolves exist?" thought the pirate,
smiling to himself.
And he shouted out loud with confidence:

"They don't exist,
they don't exist,
they don't exist."

And the werewolf vanished!

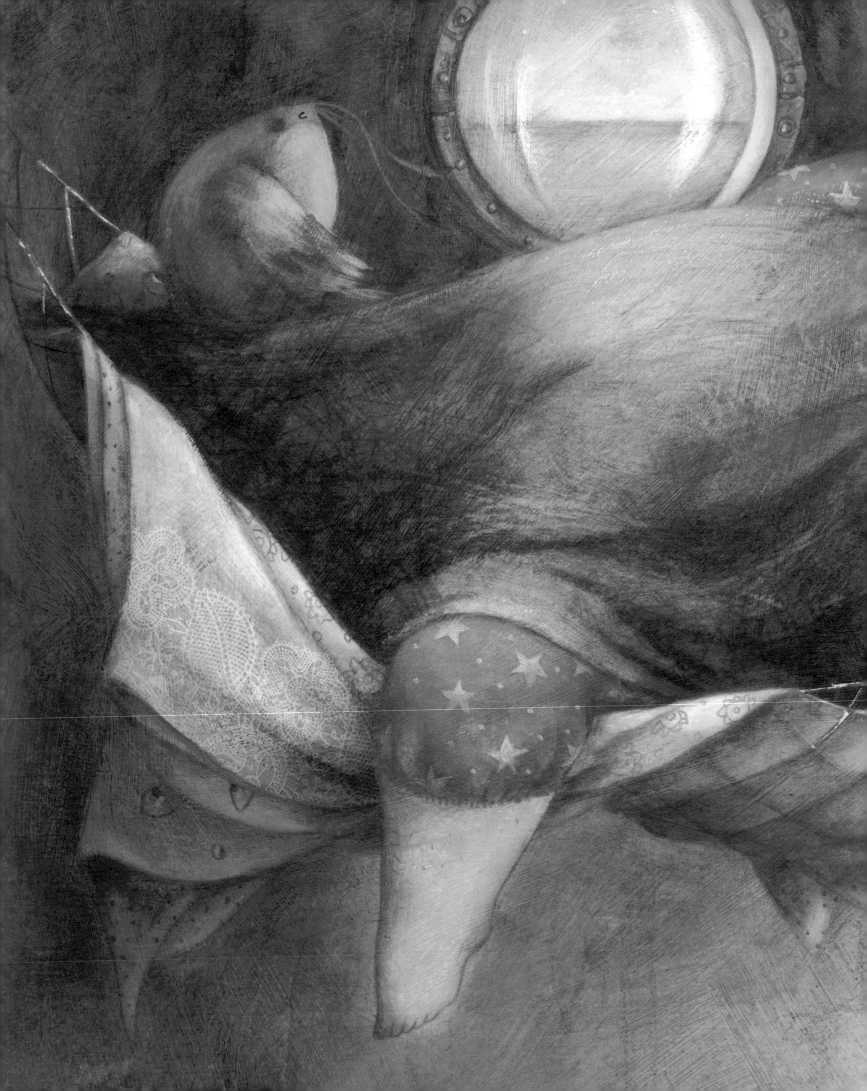

Tired, satisfied, and with no fear left,
Captain Scaredy Cat decided to go to sleep.

He made the bed with

blue-eyed sheets,

covered himself with a black cape,

and hugged his
teddy wolf.

And from that night on,

Captain Scaredy Cat

slept peacefully

and was never ever afraid again.

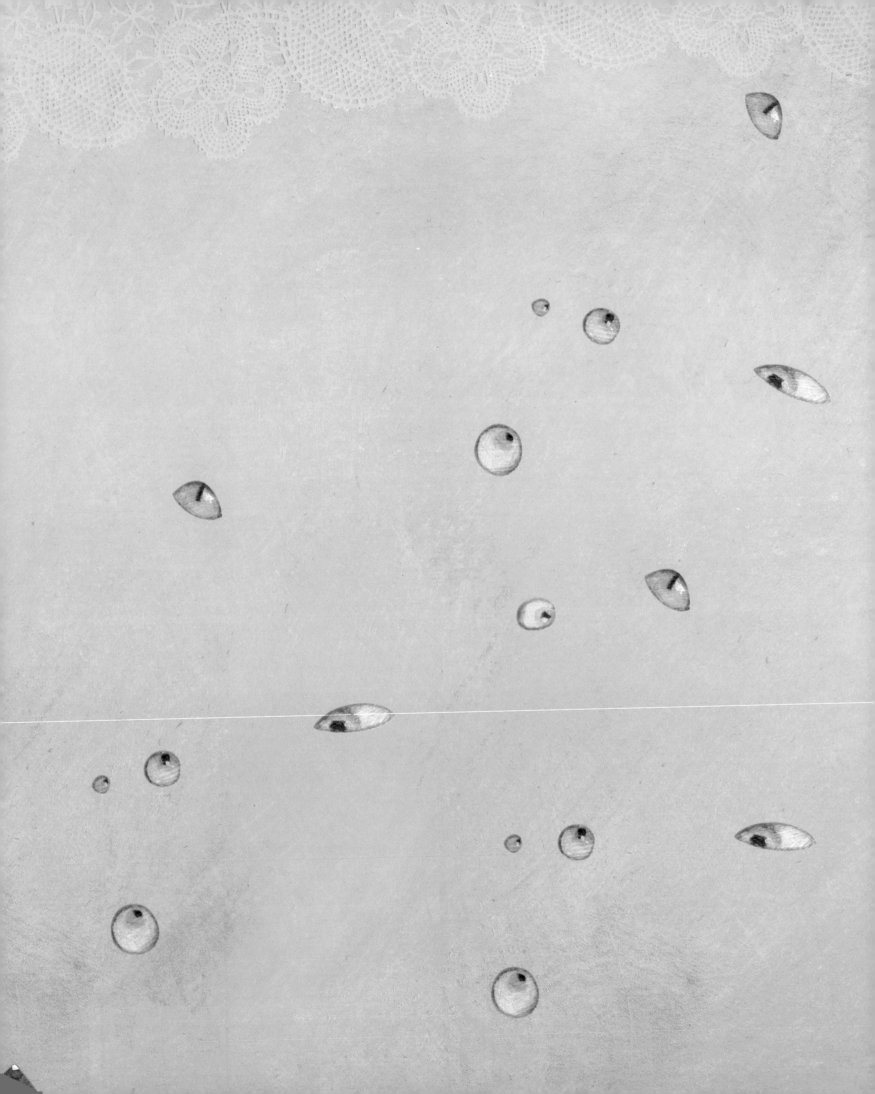